Disney's POCAHONTAS
Painting with the Wind

A BOOK ABOUT COLORS

by Teddy Slater

Illustrated by Ed Ghertner and Del Thompson

Disney
PRESS

NEW YORK

First Edition
13 5 7 9 10 8 6 4 2

Library of Congress Catalog Card Number 94-71797
ISBN 0-7868-3041-7 / 0-7868-5031-0 (lib. bdg.)

Disney's POCAHONTAS
Painting with the Wind
A BOOK ABOUT COLORS

Yellow is the color of the autumn leaves that ride the whirling wind.

"Pocahontas," they whisper as they fall. "Catch us if you can."

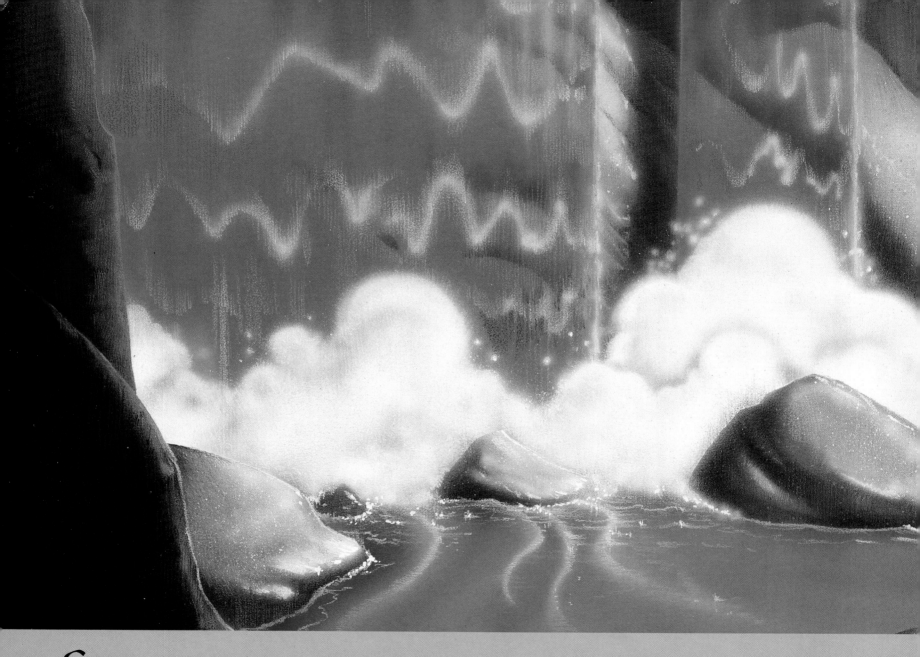

"Come wade with me in the swift-flowing stream," Pocahontas calls to John Smith.

"Come feel the cool blue water."

By the edge of the stream rests a hollow brown log.

Meeko stops to explore—and sends a squirrel scurrying.

Pocahontas gives John a gift of sweet berries—

juicy, plump, and very purple.

Hovering over the fragrant pink flowers,

Flit drinks his fill of nectar.

An orange blur of butterflies swoops across the sky.

The biggest one comes fluttering down . . . and lands on Meeko's nose!

John stretches out on a green, grass carpet

to bask in the warmth of the sun.

"Welcome, little red bird," says Grandmother Willow.

"There's room for your nest in my branches."

Silvery gray clouds go drifting by.

Shadows creep over the land.

As the colors of the wind fade into night,

a white moon lights up the sky.